THE BEST TRICK OF ALL

First Steck-Vaughn Edition 1992

Copyright © 1989 American Teacher Publications

Published by Steck-Vaughn Company

Library of Congress number: 89-3660

Library of Congress Cataloging in Publication Data.

Dale, Nora.
  The best trick of all / Nora Dale; illustrated by Roberta Holmes-Landers.

  (Real readers)
  Summary: Four clowns have a contest to see who can do the best trick.
  [1. Clowns—Fiction. 2. Stories in rhyme.] I. Holmes-Landers, Roberta, ill. II. Title.
III. Series.
  PZ8.3.D158Be   1989   [E]—dc19   89-3660

ISBN 0-8172-3505-1   hardcover library binding

ISBN 0-8114-6700-7   softcover binding

    5 6 7 8 9 0   96

The Best Trick of All

by Nora Dale

illustrated by
Roberta Holmes-Landers

STECK-VAUGHN
C O M P A N Y
A Subsidiary of National Education Corporation

All the clowns have a trick
That they think they do well,
But they want Jo to pick,
And they want Jo to tell:

What is the best trick
Of the tricks that they do?
What trick would you pick
If the clowns came to you?

"On the top of this ball
I can ride on a bike!
Do you think I will fall?
No, no, not me!" said Mike.

"If you want to see tricks,
Then I think you will see
That the best trick of all
Is the one done by me!"

"Oho!" yelled out Nan.
"That trick is a treat.
But I think my trick can
Take the socks off your feet!"

Nan said, "See my hat?
It may not look big.
But you see—just like that!
I can take out a pig!

"If you want to see tricks,
Then I think you will see
That the best trick of all
Is the one done by me!"

"Oho!" yelled out Bea.
"That trick is just fine.
But I think you will see
That the best trick is mine!"

"I can play on a drum
On the top of my head.
See me play TUM TEE TUM
RUM TUM TUM TEE!" Bea said.

"If you want to see tricks,
Then I think you will see
That the best trick of all
Is the one done by me!"

"Oho!" yelled out Nick.
"That trick is just fine.
But the trick you will pick
For the best trick is mine!"

Nick said, "I've a bat
On the top of my head,
And on top of that
Is a ball that is red!

"If you want to see tricks,
Then I think you will see
That the best trick of all
Is the one done by me!"

"Oho!" yelled out Jo.
"All the tricks can't be beat!
We can put on a show
That will be a big treat!"

Here is Mike on a bike,
And a pig in a hat,
And a drum you will like,
And a ball on a bat!

If you like to see tricks,
Here is where you can go.
For the best tricks of all
Are the ones in this show!

Sharing the Joy of Reading

Beginning readers enjoy reading books on their own. Reading a book is a worthwhile activity in and of itself for a young reader. However, a child's reading can be even more rewarding if it is shared. This sharing can enhance your child's appreciation—both of the book and of his or her own abilities.

Now that your child has read **The Best Trick of All**, you can help extend your child's reading experience by encouraging him or her to:

- Retell the story or key concepts presented in this story in his or her own words. The retelling can be oral or written.

- Create a picture of a favorite character, event, or concept from this book.

- Express his or her own ideas and feelings about the characters in this book and other things the characters might do.

Here is an activity you can do together to help extend your child's appreciation of this book: Like the circus clowns in the story, your child might enjoy performing a simple trick. Start by helping your child think of a trick, such as balancing a book on top of the head, or throwing a ball in the air and clapping hands before catching it. Supply the appropriate equipment and supervise your child while he or she practices the trick. Once your child has mastered the trick, he or she might like to wear clown make-up and perform the trick for other family members or friends.